SPORTS
KE
N
KS

KNUCKLEHEAD

SKIP PRESS

 Artesian **Press**
P.O. Box 355 Buena Park, CA 90621

Take Ten Books
Sports

Half and Half	1-58659-032-4
Cassette	1-58659-037-5
The Phantom Falcon	1-58659-031-6
Cassette	1-58659-036-7
Match Point	1-58659-035-9
Cassette	1-58659-040-5
The Big Sundae	1-58659-034-0
Cassette	1-58659-039-1
Knucklehead	**1-58659-033-2**
Cassette	**1-58659-038-?**

Other Take Ten Themes:
Mystery
Adventure
Disaster
Chillers
Thrillers
Fantasy

Project Editor:Liz Parker
Assistant Editor: Carol Newell
Cover Illustrator:Marjorie Taylor
Cover Designer: Tony Amaro
Text Illustrator:Fujiko Miller
©2000 Artesian Press

All rights reserved. No part of this publication may be reproduced or transmitted in any form without the permission in writing from the publisher. Reproduction of any part of this book, through photocopy, recording, or any electronic or mechanical retrieval system, without the written permission of the publisher is an infringement of copyright law.

ISBN 1-58659-033-?

Chapter 1

"You're bogus!" said Tommy Burns in a none-too-friendly voice. "Go back to the country where you belong!"

"There isn't any work there," Wilbert Reed replied, with anger in his voice that he wasn't hiding very well.

Peter Burns, Tommy's shorter, uglier and meaner twin brother, gave Wilbert a disgusted look. He spat on the ground so hard his giant wad of chewing gum went flying onto the grass. "If your family is as dumb as you, they couldn't get work anywhere!" Peter cried. "Learn to catch, Knucklehead!"

Wilbert looked toward home plate from his position in right field. The other baseball team was still cheering as they danced around the player who had just scored the winning run. Wilbert's team, the Bulldogs, had taken the lead earlier that inning. The game would have been over, and his Bulldogs would have won, if Wilbert had only caught the long fly ball he had just missed, by inches.

Tommy and Peter, who also played in the outfield, were trotting off toward the home team dugout now, still complaining angrily about Wilbert's big goof. Wilbert took off his worn old baseball glove and started off, wondering how many more angry insults he would have to listen to. He ran his first few steps, then began walking, his head bowed. At least his mother had been working and missed seeing him goof up.

The clubhouse was the same one used during football season, and the lockers were made of wood and wire screen, to get more air to the dirty, smelly uniforms. Wilbert tried to get to his locker without being noticed, but it was impossible. Some of his junior high school teammates were still angry. He saw them through the wire walls of their lockers, sitting on the wooden benches, shooting mean glances his way or turning their faces from him as they went to take a shower.

Only Ernie Cannon, the equipment manager, was his usual cheerful self. Ernie was a short, wiry kid with black-rimmed glasses that made him look smart. Unlike the other teenagers, Ernie's big goal was to be a big-league umpire, then one day own a major league baseball team.

Wilbert wasn't sure how Ernie could achieve both of those goals without winning the state lottery a couple of times, but he liked Ernie a lot. Ernie was the only kid who had gone out of his way to befriend Wilbert when his family moved to town only a month before.

"The stats were against you, kid," Ernie said, placing a consoling hand on his friend's back. Wilbert was at least six inches taller than Ernie, but Ernie said "kid" like he was much older and wiser. "Brock was way overdue. He's a power hitter, and he hadn't really tagged one the last couple of games." Brock was the player who hit the fly ball that Wilbert had missed.

"I don't need stats, Ernie," Wilbert replied. "I need to catch the ball when it counts."

"You're wastin' your brain on him, Cannon." It was Tommy Burns, naked except for a towel wrap, on his way to the showers.

"Yeah," chimed in Peter Burns, dressed just like his twin. "Bet he doesn't even know what stats are."

"Statistics!" Wilbert barked, his shame over losing the game quickly fading into a growing rage.

"Knucklehead!"

Peter stopped in his tracks and faced Wilbert, ready for a fight. Wilbert rose, his shirt hanging open to reveal his skinny chest. Wilbert glanced down at his open uniform then at the stockily built Peter. The Burns boys had their own exercise and weight equipment at home. They were always talking about "bulking up" and things like that.

Everything the Burns boys owned was top of the line, from the sunglasses that snapped onto their caps down to the expensive cleated baseball shoes they wore. Wilbert was poor, but strong despite his thin body, due to years of working on a farm. Still, he wondered now if he was a match for Peter, particularly with Tommy looking ready to fight, too.

"Hey, it was a joke," Wilbert said, a lump in his throat.

"I'll tell you what isn't a joke," Tommy declared. "We're gonna get you if you keep messin' up, Knucklehead."

"Yeah," echoed Peter, "we might even hire someone to get you for us." He looked at his twin and grinned. "We'll hire a hit man!"

"Yeah!" Tommy responded. "A hit man!"

"Why don't both of you boys go take a shower and think about the hits *you* missed!"

It was a snarled command, not a question. It was Coach Rogers, his cap pushed back on his thinning hairline. The Burns boys turned and hurried off to the showers without a word. "Those boys have short memories," said Coach.

"And sick minds," said Ernie.

"Don't pay any attention to 'em, Wilbert. If either one of 'em had done anything but strike out in the eighth inning, we would have had another run. And if we had had another pitcher it would have made a big difference."

Wilbert went back to getting his uniform off, feeling embarrassed. Coach Rogers stood there for a moment, then put one foot on the bench and leaned toward Wilbert.

"I sure wish you had picked up a pair of sunglasses like I suggested, Wilbert," he said quietly.

Ernie cleared his throat and caught Coach's eyes. Ernie pointed at his own pocket. Wilbert looked at Ernie painfully, then out a window, now even more embarrassed. Ernie knew something Coach didn't. The Reeds had moved to the city not because there was no work in the country—they had lost their farm to foreclosure after Wilbert's father died in an accident.

Coach Rogers nodded in sudden understanding. Wilbert obviously couldn't afford a new pair of flip-down shades. "Well, maybe I can take care of those sunglasses," Coach announced.

He cleared his throat and sat down on the bench. "Wilbert, you have a strong arm, and you hit pretty good, but not when you let this zero confidence thing get to you. Show up here tomorrow afternoon. There are some things I want to go over with you."

Before Wilbert could work up the courage to ask what was so important they had to go over it on a Saturday, Coach Rogers went into his office and shut the door. Wilbert raised an eyebrow at Ernie, who shrugged and walked away.

Wilbert killed time cleaning the dirt off his cleats, waiting until the Burns boys were gone before taking his shower. By the time he came back to the locker room, all of the other players had left, too. As he dressed, he watched through the big glass window of Coach's office, where Coach was going over the charts Ernie kept on each game. Coach kept shaking his head, and Ernie kept chattering away and pointing at the charts.

Without waiting for his friend, Wilbert slipped out the door and headed up some steps to the street. He had lots of patience, from years of raising crops. He knew, somehow, that they could still find a way to win the championship that seemed so important to everyone in Chambersburg. He took a deep breath, hoping that everyone would forget about today's game. And what about his upcoming meeting with Coach? Oh, brother. Then, feeling a presence, he stopped suddenly and looked up.

There, at the top of the steps, was a broad-bodied, mean-looking man with grayish hair, looking down at him with deep furrows in his brow. "Want to talk to you about the game, kid," growled the man in a deep voice. "You got a minute?"

Chapter 2

Wilbert just stood there, scared to death, unable to say a word.

"Moses Walker," said the big man, putting a huge hand out in Wilbert's direction.

"It was just one game!" Wilbert squeaked, backing down the steps. "Whatever the Burns boys are paying you, I'll pay you twice as much to leave me alone!" He gulped. "I swear!"

Moses Walker frowned. "What do you think I am, boy, a hit man or something?"

Wilbert stood against a wall, nodding fearfully.

Moses began to chuckle, then he began to laugh out loud. He was still laughing when Ernie came running up the steps.

"Hey, Moses, did I miss a good joke?" Ernie asked.

Moses was chuckling now. He pointed to Wilbert and laughed.

"You know this guy?" Wilbert asked.

"Sure," Ernie shrugged. "Moses is probably the Bulldogs' biggest fan. Comes to every game he can." Ernie glanced down at his watch, then let out a whistle. "Wow, I'm late! See ya! See ya later, Moses!" With that, he was off and running up the steps.

Wilbert began to laugh. He might have known. The Burns boys were mostly talk when it came to threats.

"Come with me, son," Moses said. "Let's talk some baseball."

Moses explained the situation as they walked. He had been watching Wilbert play. Wilbert's catching needed work, but he had a great arm. Moses wondered if Wilbert might do better at another position than outfielder. "Ever try pitching?" Moses asked.

It was getting near sunset, and they were walking on the railroad tracks that split the small town of Chambersburg. Wilbert looked ahead to the intersection where Bascomb's Hardware already displayed a "Closed" sign. In another couple of hours, his mother would be getting home from her job at the mobile home factory that the Burns family owned. She was working overtime today.

"Well, I pitched in Little League back home, but since we've been here, I don't have very good control," Wilbert said after a moment. He was walking on the rail, trying not to lose his balance. "I used to knock squirrels out of trees with rocks, back in the country." He shook his head. "I guess I just lost the touch."

Moses looked down at the gravel between the railroad ties crunching beneath his feet and nodded thoughtfully. "Listen," he said. "I used to play pro ball. Maybe I could work with you on your control. When do you have time?"

Wilbert looked up sharply. A former professional ballplayer wanted to teach him pitching? Wow! "I have some time right now," he announced. "Where do you live?"

Moses pointed up ahead, on the east side of the tracks. "Over yonder a couple of blocks."

"You're just across the train tracks from me!" Wilbert grinned. "Hey, Mr. Walker, let's go!"

Moses lived in a well-kept house with a covered front porch, a garden to one side and a yard with a big shade tree out back. Moses' dog, Bear, was a large black, wiry-haired Bouvier d'Flandres, a breed Wilbert had never seen before. Bear was like Moses; he looked tough and mean, but he was great once you got to know him. Moses went into a tool shack in one corner of the backyard and came out with a home plate, which he set up near the back of his house. He went inside the house, then returned with a catcher's mitt and a bag of old baseballs. After Moses marked off the proper throwing distance with a wooden stake, he stood at the back of the house and motioned for Wilbert to start pitching.

Wilbert threw, all right. Some were very fast, fast enough to cause a loud *smack* when they hit Moses' glove, but not many of them were in the area of the plate. Bear would retrieve any balls that Moses didn't catch and seemed never to tire of helping out.

"Relax, kid!" Moses kept yelling.

Wilbert kept trying to relax, but his arm just seemed to get tighter. Then Moses began telling country jokes, like the one about the three-legged hog who

saved the farmer's life. Wilbert started
to laugh, but Moses wouldn't let him
stop throwing. It seemed the more
Wilbert laughed, the better his pitching
got. Pretty soon, he was getting almost
every pitch over the plate.

By the time Moses was ready to
quit, the sun was just about down.
They sat in the wide swing on Moses'
front porch, drinking lemonade and
talking about baseball.

"Guess I've just been too wound up,
huh, Moses?"

Moses nodded. He sipped at his
lemonade and looked off toward the
setting sun. "Wilbert, you ever hear of
Stun 'Em Stovey?"

"Nope. Was he famous?" Wilbert
looked toward Bear, who was drinking
lemonade from his bowl.

"Yeah, he was famous," Moses replied. "He was a pitcher, a star of the
old Negro Leagues. And he was my
grandfather."

"What was the Negro Leagues?" Wilbert asked, still looking at Bear, who had finished off the big bowl of lemonade and was now looking at Wilbert's glass. Wilbert quickly finished his drink.

"Way back before you were born, nobody but white people played major league baseball, so the African-American people put together their own teams. My grandpa was one of the greatest spitball pitchers of all time. You could learn a lot from his example."

Wilbert almost choked on the last gulp of lemonade. "Spitball? You can't throw spitballs, Moses! They're illegal."

Moses gave Wilbert a stern look. "Don't you think I know that?" Wilbert nodded. "No, Grandpa Stovey's problem was that he got all uptight about things, and it messed up his playing. Then he learned a special pitch that took him far, but first he had to learn to relax." Moses reached over to Bear's bowl and poured the rest of his glass of lemonade into it. Bear immediately started lapping it up as if he was dying of thirst.

Both Moses and Wilbert burst out laughing.

"Well, I better go walk all this lemonade off Bear," Moses said, getting up from the porch swing. "We can talk tomorrow."

"I gotta meet Coach Rogers at the field," Wilbert said, feeling a little disappointed. "Sunday, maybe?"

Moses nodded and said nothing more. He just grabbed Bear's leash off a nail by the front door and led the dog off for a walk.

Wilbert was deep in thought as he hurried down off the railroad tracks onto the road leading to his house. He was so busy thinking about what had gone on at Moses' house that he barely noticed the Burns brothers come up on their mountain bikes.

"Hey, Knucklehead!" shouted Peter. "Think about quitting yet?"

"Might be a good idea!" yelled Tommy.

"What do you guys want, a fight?" Wilbert asked. He dropped his glove in the dirt and doubled up his fists. "Come on, I'll take you, one at a time!"

The Burns boys looked at each other and grinned. They both got off their bikes. Wilbert took a deep breath. He hated to fight, but he wasn't going to back down—not this time. Then, to his surprise, the Burns boys climbed back on their bikes and took off. He stood there a moment, dumbfounded. Then he heard a bark. He whirled around and saw Bear, Moses' Bouvier d'Flandres, standing beside Moses, his teeth bared.

"That's enough, Bear!" Moses commanded. Bear instantly relaxed, and barked out a greeting. "Keep working on relaxing," Moses told Wilbert. "Things work out better that way."

Chapter 3

No matter how much he concentrated on staying relaxed, Wilbert felt the muscles in his back tightening as he walked into the clubhouse that Saturday morning. Without saying a word, Coach Rogers handed him a gift—a pair of flip-down sunglasses.

"Uh, Coach. We're just gettin' on our feet. We'll pay …"

Too late. Coach was out the door, carrying a bat and a bag of baseballs. Wilbert clipped the sunglasses onto the brim of his cap and followed Coach outside.

They practiced fielding all morning, with Coach hitting one tall fly ball after another to Wilbert. The sunglasses made a big difference, Wilbert discovered. He got used to flipping the glasses down the minute he heard the crack of the ball against the bat. Still, he dropped more flies than he should have, because Coach spent a good deal of time inquiring into Wilbert's family life, which was the last thing in the world Wilbert needed to talk about if he wanted to stay relaxed.

"My father was never the same when the farm went broke," Wilbert explained as they took a break. Coach Rogers had brought along a small cooler of sodas, and they had both downed most of the bottles pretty quickly. "It wasn't two months later ..." Wilbert paused, his throat getting tight. "Well," he continued, "the sheriff just showed up at the door one night and said Dad had been killed in a car accident. It was raining and stuff that night. Dad didn't even have any life insurance."

Wilbert lowered his head and wiped back the tears. Coach patted Wilbert's shoulder a couple of times.

"That's okay, kid," said Coach. "Sorry. I didn't know."

Wilbert looked up quickly. "You wouldn't tell ..."

"No, I won't tell anybody. But I'll tell you one thing. After this morning, I've changed my mind about putting you on the bench. I think those sunglasses made all the difference."

Wilbert beamed. "No kiddin', Coach?"

"No kiddin', Wilbert."

"You're wasting your time," came a deep voice.

Wilbert and Coach looked around at the same time. Sitting behind them in the stands was Moses Walker, his dog Bear sitting silently at his side. Coach Rogers pushed back his cap and nodded to Moses, who nodded back.

"What do you mean I'm wasting my time?" Coach asked.

Wilbert thought he heard more than just a touch of anger in the Coach's voice.

"I mean Wilbert isn't an outfielder. This boy is Babe Ruth, but a pitcher not a hitter. He ought to go from the outfield to pitching."

Coach Rogers frowned at Wilbert as if trying to make sense of what Moses had said. He looked back at Moses. "How do you figure?"

"I'm sayin' he's a pitcher, Gerald. A good one."

"You guys know each other?" Wilbert asked, surprised.

Coach Rogers turned red. He looked off toward the clubhouse. "I gotta go make a phone call. See you at practice, kid." Without looking back, Coach Rogers picked up his bat and started off.

Wilbert watched Coach until he was inside the clubhouse. Then he turned and found Moses standing by his side, with Bear holding a catcher's mitt in his teeth. "Hey, Moses," Wilbert said, "how do you know Coach?"

"We go back a ways," Moses replied. It was apparently all he wanted to say, because he took the catcher's mitt from Bear and stood behind home plate. "Grab some balls and start throwing." Moses sat down behind the plate. He squatted on his left leg and stuck his right leg out in front. For the first time, Wilbert saw that Moses had a dummy leg. "Quit gawkin' and get to pitchin'!" Moses demanded. He turned to the dog. "Bear! Balls, Bear!"

It was the same routine from the day before, only this time on a real baseball diamond. Wilbert decided to not ask any more questions. Moses was giving him expert tips and keeping him relaxed with jokes. Bear happily chased after any balls that got away and brought them back to Wilbert.

"Stop throwing with just your arm and shoulder!" Moses yelled. "Get your whole body into it!" Then he would demonstrate. "No, no! You're holding it wrong! Hold the ball across the wide seams!" Again, Moses showed him, and Wilbert got it right.

Then Moses let a ball go by without even trying to catch it. He stood up and started toward Wilbert, a very serious look on his face. He was pounding his glove with a fist.

"What did I do wrong?" Wilbert asked nervously.

"I think you can do it right now," Moses said. "Yessir, I thought for a while I was wrong, but I bet you can do it. I'm gonna teach you that special pitch my Grandpa taught me."

"But, Moses, I told you! Spitballs are illegal!"

"Knuckleballs aren't," Moses said quietly. "At least not yet."

Moses showed Wilbert how to throw a knuckleball, pushing the ball out of his palm with his fingertips on the release. Moses even pulled out a nail file and filed Wilbert's nails so that they were straight across instead of rounded, making it easier to throw the pitch.

All of a sudden, Wilbert realized he was getting hungry. He looked up in the sky, and saw that it was well into the afternoon, maybe three o'clock.

As if sensing what was on Wilbert's mind, Moses picked himself up and checked his watch. "3:34," he called out. "Man, if I hadn't seen it with my own eyes, I wouldn't believe it. You're a natural knuckleballer, Wilbert. I ain't seen nothin' like it since ... well, in a long time."

Wilbert grinned, knowing that Moses was right. He really could pitch. And the knuckleball! When he got it right, the ball switched between hopping and gliding to the plate. If he could throw it in a game, no one could hit it!

"That was great!" Wilbert pounded Moses' arm enthusiastically. He started to slap Moses' arm again, then heard a snappish growl. He looked down and saw Bear, his teeth bared. "Sorry!" he yelled, quickly pulling his hand back from Moses.

Moses laughed. "Don't worry 'bout Bear. He's just real protective of me. I've had him since he was a little puppy. He was just showing you not to get too carried away. Besides, you take it easy on that throwing hand. And keep those nails filed."

"Yo!" Wilbert responded. He pulled off his baseball cap and scratched the back of his head. "So you think I've got it, Moses?"

"I think you got a chance to get it," came the answer. "Just remember to stay relaxed. Take it a step at a time—and practice."

Before Wilbert could say much more, Moses said good-bye and went off, limping slightly after his magnificent dog. Wilbert began walking toward the clubhouse, then realized that it was Saturday. The clubhouse door was closed. The Coach had probably left already. Then he remembered the baseballs he'd left on the field, and turned back to get them.

Wilbert turned and saw Coach Rogers standing in the now open doorway of the clubhouse. "Coach! Thought you were gone."

"Nope. I was watching you. You really can throw, can't you?"

Wilbert grinned. "Yeah, long as I stay relaxed. I guess it's like you're always saying. It's the little things—fundamentals."

"Right. Listen, you don't lose those 'fundamental' sunglasses I gave you, all right?"

Wilbert reached quickly toward the brim of his hat, then breathed a sigh of relief. The flip-downs were still there. "You bet, Coach. Hey, thanks again. I'll pay you for them when ..."

"Forget it. Help somebody else out, one of these days."

"Okay." Wilbert jerked a thumb toward the ball field. "I was gonna go back and round up the balls." He turned to go.

"Wilbert."

He turned back. Coach had a serious look on his face. "Yeah, Coach, what is it?"

"I'll go catch a few with you. I was watching you throw from the clubhouse. I think I might want to try you out as pitcher next week."

Chapter 4

To the surprise of everyone, including himself, Wilbert was turning in a fantastic performance in his first outing as a Bulldog pitcher. Even Tommy Burns mumbled a compliment at the seventh inning stretch. At least Wilbert thought it sounded like a compliment; it was hard to hear when everyone in the stands was singing "Take Me Out to the Ball Game."

Peter Burns, on the other hand, had been calling Wilbert "Knucklehead" every chance he got: "Try and get a hit this time, Knucklehead." "Keep it high with this Blue Jay, Knucklehead. Didn't you hear Coach say he's a low ball hitter?" "Where'd you say you learned to throw, Knucklehead?"

Now it was the ninth inning, and there was one out. The Bulldogs were one run ahead. If Wilbert got the next two batters out, he'd win the game. Trouble was, his main pitch, the fastball, had been losing power, and his arm was sore. He thought about using the knuckleball, but he wasn't confident enough to try it.

Steve Wilson, the Bulldogs' chubby catcher, was supposed to be on the pitcher's mound discussing the game plan with Wilbert. Instead, Steve was telling a joke. Steve reached the punch line and let out a big laugh, but Wilbert just smiled politely. "What's the matter, don't you think it's funny?"

"Heard it before, Steve. Sorry."

"Okay, just trying to loosen you up. Let's get these guys out, okay? Keep trying your curve. They're not expecting it."

Steve went back toward home plate,

and Wilbert pounded his glove with the ball. He looked over at Coach Rogers, who was standing at the edge of the dugout. Coach nodded his head, signalling he was keeping Wilbert in. Wilbert turned, took the signal from Steve, and threw the next pitch, wide of the plate—so wide Steve had to chase after it. Wilbert took a long, deep breath. He felt his muscles tense up anyway. Three pitches later, the runner was on base, walked by four pitches nowhere near the strike zone. Wilbert saw Coach Rogers take off his cap, but he didn't come toward the mound. Neither did Steve. Wilbert faced the next batter and let it fly, this time going with the fastball.

Whack! He could barely turn fast enough to watch the ball leave the bat and sail over the fence in center field. Home run. The Blue Jays were ahead by one.

When it was the Bulldogs' turn to

bat, Coach Rogers told Peter Burns to relief pitch if they went into another inning. Wilbert didn't mind. After all, Peter had a good arm. Then Peter hit a double and knocked in a couple of runs, winning the game. Wilbert winced inside, even though he was cheering because his team won. He knew he would hear about giving up the home run for a while, from Peter, if no one else. And why didn't he have enough confidence to try the knuckleball? It might have made the difference. He was the first one out of the clubhouse, giving no one a chance to say much to him.

Wilbert hurried up the steps to the parking lot, expecting Moses to be there with a comment on his performance. Instead, to his amazement, there was his mother, waiting by their car.

"Mom!" he blurted out. "Why aren't you at work?"

She frowned. "What's wrong, Wil?

Don't you want me to see you play?"

Wilbert blushed. That wasn't what he meant at all. "No, I just thought you couldn't get off work, that's all. Shoot, I'm glad. It's great you saw the game. At least, most of it."

"Coach Rogers put in a call to Mr. Burns," she explained as they climbed in their old Chevrolet. "Mr. Burns was coming to the game, and he told me to take off, too. He didn't know you played."

Wilbert was silent for a few minutes, until they were out of sight of the clubhouse. "So what did you really think?" he asked. "Think I could play pro ball one day?"

Mrs. Reed shook her head sadly. "I don't know, Wilbert. I think counting on anything like a baseball career is such a long shot. You should concentrate on getting a good education."

Wilbert sighed and looked out his window. There by the hot dog stand was Moses, feeding Bear a hot dog. Moses looked at him, held up a hand, and made the motion of throwing a knuckleball.

Chapter 5

After winning the next two games, the Bulldogs were tied for the district championship. The last game was in Townerville, and this time Wilbert's mother had to work for sure. Wilbert got the call to start the game and tried to ignore the sour look on Peter Burns' face. Because of an injury, however, Coach Rogers moved Peter in from the outfield to play shortstop, meaning Wilbert would have to listen to Peter's smart remarks the whole game. As they were about to take the field, Ernie pulled Peter aside, making sure that Wilbert was within hearing distance.

"Peter," Ernie said excitedly, "did you hear the news?"

"What news, Ernie?" Peter sounded as bored as possible. "More of your stat reports?"

"I heard there's a college scout in the stands! This game might mean a scholarship for somebody."

Suddenly Peter was interested. "You leveling with me, Ernie?"

Ernie nodded his head rapidly, keeping his crossed fingers hidden behind his back, although Wilbert saw them.

"Man!" Peter cried. "I'm battin' a thousand tonight!"

As Peter hustled onto the field, Wilbert stopped Ernie. "What was that all about?" he asked. "And why does he care about a scholarship to college? The Burns are rich."

A mean grin stole across Ernie's face. "You don't understand," he said. "Peter is so into status he's too dumb to realize that college scouts don't care about junior high!"

Wilbert and Ernie shared a laugh, which was cut short by the sudden presence of Moses Walker. He handed a big catcher's mitt to Ernie.

"What's that for?" Ernie asked.

"It's a special mitt," Moses replied. He gave Wilbert a wink. "Give it to the catcher. He's gonna need it today."

When Wilbert started throwing the knuckleball, even he was amazed at how it stunned the other team's batters. Coach Rogers freaked, but only because Steve Wilson, the catcher, was fooled by a number of the pitches, too.

No one could hit the crazy, bobbing pitch. Going into the ninth inning, Wilbert was pitching a no-hitter. Even Peter Burns was silenced.

As the game wore on, Ernie started searching frantically through *The Official Encyclopedia of Baseball,* which he kept with him at all times.

"Wow!" he exclaimed, as Wilbert was just about to go up to bat. "Guess who was the youngest knuckleballer to ever pitch a no-hitter."

Wilbert shook his head. He had no idea.

"Moses Walker," Ernie said quietly. "That blows my mind."

It must have been Wilbert's night. He got a hit on the second pitch. Peter, following him in the batting order, immediately slugged a triple. Wilbert scored. The next three batters made easy outs, however, leaving Peter stranded at third base, but the Bulldogs were on the scoreboard with a 1-0 lead.

When Wilbert started back onto the field to pitch what he hoped would be the last inning, Ernie pulled him aside.

"You gotta watch the knuckleball," Ernie cautioned. "I was over by the Tigers' dugout, picking up a bat, and I heard their coach saying 'Pop and glide, pop and glide, when you see it take your stride.'"

"So what does that mean?" Wilbert

asked. Then, as Ernie went through the motion of throwing a knuckleball, it came to him. "Must be how you hit a knuckleball, huh?"

Ernie shrugged. "I don't know, but I thought I'd warn you."

Wilbert went back to his fastball and struck out the first batter. Then he noticed Moses in the stands, clapping and cheering. He decided to strike out a batter for Moses, using the knuckleball.

The first two pitches went by the batter. Then the Tigers' coach yelled at him, and made a motion not unlike the one Ernie had made in the Bulldogs' dugout. Wilbert took the sign from Steve Wilson for a curve, then waved it off, and decided to go for the knuckleball, anyway.

At first, it looked like the batter was going to just stand there. Then, at the last possible moment, the kid crouched down and bunted.

It took everyone by surprise. Steve

Wilson fell flat on his face, scrambling to get the ball. Then he recovered, picked up the ball, and threw it well over the first baseman's head. By the time the Bulldogs got it together, the runner had advanced to third base and was in scoring position.

Coach Rogers came to the pitcher's mound for a conference. Wilbert asked him about the "pop and glide" remark, and the Coach nodded his head. "Yep, that's the way to hit a knuckleball, all right. Maybe you better lay off it and just throw some other stuff, Wilbert. Or maybe we oughta let Peter pitch?"

Wilbert looked at the eager short-stop standing near the coach. He shook his head and held on tightly to the ball. "Coach," he said quietly, "I got us this far. I can take us all the way."

Coach Rogers hesitated a moment, then grinned at Wilbert's apparently brimming confidence. He patted Wilbert on the shoulder, then turned and walked back toward the dugout.

Wilbert hung the first pitch on the inside corner for a strike. Then he looked up in the stands and saw something that shook his confidence a little. There was Moses, but who was that sitting with him? The man was wearing a college letter jacket, and a white shirt and tie. Was he a scout, after all? It would be just like Moses to get one there.

It bothered Wilbert. He threw a curve. The batter nicked it, sending a foul into the stands. The next three pitches, though, were all out of the strike zone. Now it was a "full count": two strikes and three balls. If the batter got the ball out of the infield for a hit, the man from third would score, and the Bulldogs would lose the championship.

Wilbert looked over at Coach Rogers, who nodded an okay. He was leaving it up to Wilbert to win. Wilbert

looked at Peter Burns, who was watching the silent exchange between him and the Coach.

"Don't blow it, Knucklehead!" yelled Peter.

Wilbert decided to go for it all. He was going to throw a knuckleball, whether the Tiger facing him was prepared or not. He reared back and let it go. The wobbly pitch went soaring toward the batter. The batter waited for what seemed like hours before he pulled back and took a mighty swing.

Wilbert heard the crack of the ball against the bat, then watched it rise, high into the sky above the pitcher's mound—and right into the sun. He was taking no chances. He wanted to catch this one himself, to make absolutely certain they would win.

As he ran off the pitcher's mound, he reached up to the brim of his cap to flip down his sunglasses. Then he realized with horror that he hadn't been wearing them while pitching. The ball was at the top of its arc. He could barely see it, against the sun. He looked around quickly and saw Peter Burns running in to make the catch. Peter was about to run smack into Wilbert.

"Watch out!" Wilbert yelled.

Peter took a sidestep, and they missed each other by inches. With one eye still on the ball, he shot a dumbfounded glance at Wilbert.

"It's all yours, Knucklehead!" Wilbert shouted and hurried behind Peter to back him up.

As the ball came roaring to earth, Peter dropped to his knees, and Wilbert's heart sank. It was an impossible angle to reach over and grab the ball. He closed his eyes.

The next thing he knew, the Tigers were jumping up and down. Peter had dropped the ball, and the runner from third had scored, winning the game. The district championship was lost.

Chapter 6

After they had finished dressing in the locker room, Wilbert started toward the bus with Ernie and Coach Rogers. They were both trying to buoy his spirits for the game he had pitched.

Waiting by the bus were Moses and the man who had been sitting with him in the stands.

Moses introduced his guest as Coach Bill Mead, from the University of Texas Longhorns, who had won more than their share of college baseball championships. Even Ernie was impressed when the coach told Wilbert the Longhorns would be keeping their eyes on him.

Still, Wilbert was upset at having

lost the championship. Peter and Tommy Burns, who had just come up, looked even more disappointed.

"Boys," Coach Mead offered, "Lemme tell ya'll a story that might help you out. It's about making the best of what you have. And working together with the people you have around you."

The coach told a story of two boys who had grown up as rivals, then found themselves as roommates when they reached professional baseball. They had been driving together one rainy night and began arguing. There was a wreck in an intersection, and one of the men had been injured badly, cutting short his professional career.

"I was the one who was hurt," Moses said, finishing the story.

"I was driving the car," Coach Rogers said, his voice choking a little, "and doing most of the bad-mouthing."

"Jeez," Wilbert said, not quite sure

what to say. "My worries don't seem so big, all of a sudden."

"That's the point," Moses said. "There's always a way to work things out, before it's too late."

Wilbert looked over at Peter, who was looking at the ground. He looked back at Moses and smiled. "Hey," Wilbert said. "If you didn't feel that way, you'd have to be a knucklehead."